The Book Boyfrie

By Karli Perri

Other books by Karli Perrin -
April Showers (April, #1)
April Fools (April, #2)
The Gift - short story
The Honey Trap

Find Karli -
Facebook - @authorkarliperrin
Instagram - @karliperrinauthor
Twitter - @karli_perrin
Goodreads.com/karliperrin
karliperrinauthor@hotmail.com

Dedication

To my fellow book lovers.

Chapter One

"Who do you think we should visit first?" Halle asks excitedly, sliding her table plan in front of me.

I wiggle my finger around in the air before pointing to a random author. "Jodi…Ellie…" I squint. "It's too small, I can't see what it says."

"Jodi Ellen Malpas. Good choice."

"See. I know you're still upset that Elouise dropped out but I'm a pretty good replacement, hey?" I wink. "Plus, I make an awesome book mule. Have you seen these guns?" I tense my biceps but nothing happens. "If I wasn't here, you'd have to pull your own trolley."

"That's true. Now less talking, more planning," she says, waving a pink sharpie in my face. I mock salute her. "We have a big decision to make."

"Well I'm here to help."

"Do we go clockwise or anti-clockwise around the room?"

"That's the big decision?"

"Yes. It's all in the planning."

I down the rest of my cocktail. "Jesus, I need another drink. This is life changing stuff."

She pouts. "I'm trying to be serious here."

"Okay, okay, I'm sorry. Clockwise sounds good." I order another cosmopolitan and wonder how many I'm going to need to get me through the next two days. I love my sister but when it comes to books, she can turn a little crazy. Who am I kidding? She turns batshit crazy. Jekyll and *Halle* crazy. Last night, I watched as she wrapped every single one of her books in cling film and *then* bubble wrap. I had to remind her that her books were going inside of a suitcase, not a tumble dryer. "God forbid if any of the pages fold," was her reply. Her love of books is passed down from our mother but for some reason, it skipped right past me. While Halle used to sneak out at midnight to buy the new Harry Potter books, I used to sneak out to parties or better yet, sneak boys *in*. Ten years later and not much has changed. Halle is still queuing up for books and I'm still getting my heart broken by immature men.

"Hmmm," Halle says, breaking my train of thought. "If we go clockwise, that means we won't reach Tillie until last and I'll die if I don't get to meet her. I've brought twelve books for her to sign."

"Twelve? Jesus Christ, she's going to file a restraining order against you."

"Twelve isn't that many. My friend Tracy is bringing twenty-five for one author."

"Where did you meet her? Stalkers anonymous?"

She feigns laughter. "Are you actually going to help or just make fun of me?"

"A bit of both. Why don't you go to see your favourite authors first and then just wait and see which queues are the shortest tomorrow?"

She almost chokes on her water. I tried persuading her to have a cocktail but apparently she needs to have a clear head for the signing tomorrow. "Are you joking?" she asks, eyes bugging out of her head. "There are going to be over three hundred people in the room. I can't go in there without a plan. Plus, I need to pack my trolley in order of the authors I'm going to visit. I'm stupid for leaving it this late. I was going to do it with Elouise last week but then she cancelled and I just haven't been in the mood."

"Just go clockwise and stop stressing out. This is supposed to be a fun weekend, remember?"

"Oh my god!" Halle whispers as she pulls on my arm. "Don't look now but Jackson Price just walked in!" I turn around and lock eyes with a blonde, bearded, delight of a man. He has to be at least six foot two and his arms are probably thicker than my legs. "I told you not to look," Halle whispers. "Just act normal."

"*You* act normal," I tell her as I turn back around.

She takes a deep breath and flattens her hair down. "It's weird seeing him in real life."

"Who is he?"

"Who is he? *Who is he?*"

"Is he an author?" I don't know why but I'm compelled to turn back around. Sure enough, he's still looking at me but this time he has his head leaning to one side as though he's assessing me. After a few seconds, his eyes begin to work their way south. I regret wearing my push-up bra when a slow smile spreads across his face. I narrow my eyes which makes him laugh.

"Do you think we should go over there and talk to him?"

"No," I reply bluntly.

"Why not?"

"Because he seems like an arrogant arsehole." An insanely *hot* arrogant arsehole. The good-looking ones are always the worst.

She laughs. "Oh, he is, but we love him for it."

"Who's *we*?"

"Romance readers around the world. Everybody is going to be fighting over him at the signing."

"Are you ever going to tell me who he is?"

"He's a cover model. He's like the go-to guy for romance covers. But he's better known as The Book Boyfriend."

I roll my eyes. "The Book Boyfriend?"

"He used to date an author and when they broke up, she wrote their story. The good, the bad and the ugly. Once people found out that it was based on her real life, they went crazy over it. It hit all the bestseller lists and stayed there for weeks. People started calling him The Book Boyfriend because, well, he's a real-life book boyfriend."

"Why did they break up?"

"They lived together in America but he moved over here to work."

"So she didn't want to do the long distance thing?"

"No, she was fine with long distance."

"Then what?"

"She met somebody else."

I raise my eyebrow. "She cheated?"

"No. She broke things off with Jackson first."

"Oh, how considerate of her."

Halle laughs. "You need to read the book to get the full story."

"No thanks, I'm pretty sure I have all the information I need."

"Stop with the judgy eyes. It's real life. Shit happens. She didn't *want* to fall in love with another man."

"I'm guessing Jackson didn't want her to either. Is she still with the other guy?"

"Nobody knows. She refuses to talk about it. At least we don't have to wait long for book two, it's out early next year."

"She's writing a sequel?" I ask, shocked.

"Of course she is. She'd be stupid not to. It's one of the most anticipated books of next year. Lionsgate have recently bought the rights to turn it into a movie."

"I wonder how Jackson feels about all of it."

"I don't know. Apparently, she offered him a cut but he declined."

"Wow. If that were me, I would bleed the bastard dry." I turn around to look for him but this time he's gone. It's funny how your feelings for somebody can change in a matter of minutes. "Well now I feel bad for the guy." I wink. "I guess he's a dick for a reason."

Halle laughs then looks smug as she says, "Never judge a book by its cover."

Chapter Two

We're the first ones inside the signing room. Of course Halle bought VIP tickets and of course she made us queue up outside the room an hour before the doors even opened. "Do you remember the plan?" she asks me, pulling me to the side.

"Yes, I remember the plan. You've told me at least ten times this morning."

"Talk me through it one last time."

You'd think we were about to meet the Queen. "I'm going to see the cover models first." She nods. "I'll get your books signed, flirt with all of them and then invite them for a drink and wait for you at the bar. Job done."

Her eyes nearly pop out of her head. "Zara, stop it."

I laugh. "You need to relax. I'm getting scribbles off the hot guys and then I'm going to collect your pre-orders from the three authors you've highlighted in pink."

She nods. "Good. Call me if there are any problems."

"Halle, we're in the same room. I can just come and find you. I could probably even shout you."

"Don't shout, you'll embarrass me."

"*I'll* embarrass *you?*"

"Don't forget to put the books back inside the bubble wrap pouches as soon as they've been signed."

I laugh. "Now I know why Elouise cancelled."

She ignores me and walks away, heading in the direction of the ticketed authors. I sigh then make my way over to the cover models. They have two tables between the four of them. Three guys are standing up, chatting to some other VIP's but the fourth guy, who I now know as Jackson Price, is sitting down with his phone glued to his ear. He stands up as soon as he spots me and puts his phone inside his pocket. He swaggers over to me and I find myself holding my breath. "Want to know something crazy?" he asks, skipping any kind of formal greeting.

"I have a feeling you're about to tell me."

"I was just sitting there thinking about you and then the doors opened and you were the first person to walk in. Talk about the law of attraction."

Talk about cheesy. "How many women are you going to say that to today?"

"It's not a line, it's the truth."

"Now that's a line in itself. You didn't have to end your phone call because of me."

"I wasn't on a call. As soon as I saw you, I just pretended that I was so I didn't have to talk to anybody else. You started walking over here but then stopped."

"Yeah, my sister called an impromptu staff meeting."

"Staff?"

"I'm her servant."

He laughs. "What's the pay like?"

"It's a voluntary position which I'm now regretting."

"Why don't you come and work for me instead?" He raises one eyebrow. "I'll make it worth your while."

I'm pretty sure I know where this is heading. "Let me guess, you'll pay me in sexual favours?"

His eyes go wide. "I was going to offer you a real wage but sexual favours work fine for me. Can you start immediately?"

"I haven't even accepted."

"Do you need some time to think about it?"

"Nope."

He takes a step closer to me. "Let me reassure you that there are plenty of perks to the job. A hardworking boss, extremely *flexible* hours and lots of rewards. You'll be left satisfied at the end of every day."

"Are you finished?"

"Oh, you'll know when I've finished."

I ignore him as I place Halle's bag onto the table and root around for the one where he's half naked on the cover. I try not to let his ridiculously tanned and toned body affect me as I take it out of the bubble wrap pouch and hand it over to him. "Can you sign this for my sister?"

"Of course." He removes the post-it note with Halle's name on and then writes her a personalised message. I glance around the room, which is starting to fill up with more VIP's.

"Where's your copy?" he asks me.

I turn back around. "I don't have one."

"Would you like to buy one?"

"No thanks. I don't read."

He points at a stack of calendars. "What about a calendar instead?"

My eyes shoot to the preview of December where he's completely naked except for a Santa's hat covering his manhood. "I'll pass."

He follows my line of sight. "Are you daydreaming about what's underneath?"

"No. I'm wondering whether anybody wore the hat afterwards."

He laughs. "I don't know but I'm pretty sure that would bring a whole new meaning to the term dickhead."

I can't help but smile. I gesture to August's preview where a half-naked woman is lying on top of him at the beach. "Is she another one of your employee's?"

"No. I don't mix business with pleasure. I haven't had an *employee* in quite some time."

"A day?"

"A lot longer."

I mock gasp. "A week? Wow."

He leans in so close that I can feel his warm breath on my skin. "You seem to be very interested in my *business*. Why is that?"

I take the book out of his hand and shove it back inside Halle's tote bag. If I don't leave now, I'll be tempted to take him up on his offer so that I can find out what *rewards* are on offer. I go to leave but he gently takes hold of my hand and places something inside it. I look down to see a post-it note with Halle's name on it. I stare at the number underneath. "Three one six?" I ask.

"My room number."

I roll my eyes. "Do you ever stop?"

"No. I go on and on and on and…"

I scrunch up the post-it note and hand it back to him. "I won't be needing this." *Tell that to your ovaries.*

"Why? Have you already memorised it?"

His laughter follows me all the way across the room.

Chapter Three

"Are you talking to me yet?" I ask Halle when we get back to the hotel room hours later.

Silence.

"I'll take that as a no then." She's still annoyed at me for not putting Jackson's book back inside its bubble wrap pouch.

"I can't believe you didn't put the book back inside the bubble wrap." *See.* "How many times did we go over it?"

I groan. "Five million times."

"Exactly."

"I'm sorry. I was distracted."

"By what? The pretty cover models?"

No. By *one* pretty cover model. "I'll make it up to you."

"How?"

"I'll buy you another copy tomorrow and get it signed."

She sighs. "No, you don't have to do that. I'll just try putting something heavy on top of it. It's only a small fold."

"It won't happen again."

"Good or I'd have to fire you."

I might have already found another employer. "Did you enjoy your day?" I ask, before my imagination runs away with me for the hundredth time today. "I feel like we hardly saw each other. The afternoon session was crazy."

Her eyes light up and a huge grin spreads across her face. "I loved it. I can't wait to do it all over again tomorrow."

The thought of doing it all over again makes me need a drink. "Do you fancy a couple of drinks down at the bar?"

"No, I'm way too tired. Room service and sleep sounds perfect."

It *does* sound appealing but then again, so does a long list of cocktails. "Okay, well I won't be long. I'll just have one drink and come back."

***

One drink turned into two and two turned into three. I was planning on going back up to get some much needed rest but the positivity and laughter in the room is truly contagious. I look around and finally understand why Halle loves coming to these events so much. The atmosphere is like nothing I've ever experienced before. It's not just a book signing; it's a gathering of like-minded people. It's a place where you can truly be yourself and make lifelong friendships while bonding over the things you love the most.

I'm completely distracted when I hear a familiar voice behind me. "I saw you watching me yesterday."

I turn around to see Jackson Price looking even more edible than he did this morning. "Excuse me?"

"Last night. You were sitting right there, mesmerised by me."

I scoff. "You were the one looking at me."

"Some random woman was staring at me. Of course I'm going to look back."

"Were my breasts staring at you too?"

"Yes. Yes, they were."

"Are you always this…forward?"

"No. Just with you. Are you always this standoffish?"

"No. Just with you."

He laughs. "Well now I feel special." He holds his hand out. "Can we start over? I'm Jackson."

I shake his hand and immediately regret it when a buzz of electricity runs throughout my entire body. "Zara."

"Nice to meet you, Zara."

"Where are your friends?"

"The other models?" I nod. "They're downstairs at the casino."

"Why aren't you with them?"

"Because I've been sitting in my room for the past two hours waiting for you to show up. When you didn't, I got bored and thought I'd come and look for you instead." He laughs when I roll my eyes. "I like you. You're different."

Oh, here we go. "How am I different?"

"Well, for a start, you're not trying to jump my bones. I love the readers at these events but it sure makes me feel like a piece of meat."

My eyes shoot to his massive biceps. Something stirs deep inside of me when he shifts in his chair, causing them to tense up. Arm veins have never looked so sexy. "Maybe you should stop being so beefy then."

He chuckles. "You're my kind of person. I knew it when I first laid eyes on you."

"You don't even know me."

"I *want* to get to know you. I can tell there's a soft centre behind that tough exterior of yours."

"Nah, my soul is black."

"I don't believe that for one second."

"Why not?"

"Because you've been hauling books around for your sister. You're at a book signing even though you don't read. That says a lot about you."

I shrug. "I'm only here because her friend dropped out last minute."

"Stop selling yourself short." I look down at my feet. If I had a penny for every time I've heard that, I would be a rich woman. "Do you want to get out of here?"

I glance back up. "And go where?"

"Anywhere you want. Let's go for a walk."

I sigh. "I don't think that's a good idea."

"Why not?"

"I'm not looking for anything serious at the moment."

He laughs. "I'm not asking you to marry me, Zara. It's just a walk."

"I…you…"

"Just spit it out."

"My sister told me about you."

"Told you what exactly? How sexy and funny I am?"

"She told me about your nickname."

He looks uncomfortable for half a second before it's replaced with a smirk. "Feel free to call me whatever you want, sweetheart."

"Do you always use humour to hide how you're really feeling?"

He leans his head to one side. "Do you always ask uncomfortable questions?"

"See, you're deflecting again."

"Okay, let's make a deal. I'll answer your questions if you answer mine."

"Deal."

He looks around. "It's loud in here. Do you want to go somewhere a little quieter?"

I raise my eyebrow. "What, like room three one six?"

"Ah, so you *did* memorise it," he says with a shit-eating grin on his face.

"Don't flatter yourself. It's three numbers. It's not exactly hard to remember."

"It could be any three numbers in any combination." He stands up and holds his hand out to me. "But yes, we can go up to my room as per your request."

I shake my head. "You're unbelievable."

"Yeah, I hear that quite a lot."

I take his hand. "It's getting late. You can walk me back to my room."

"Oh, you're inviting me to your room instead?"

Quite a few people turn to watch us as we leave together. "No further than the door," I warn him.

"Which door? The bedroom door? That's fine by me. I don't like to limit myself to a bed. I'm not very conventional in that sense."

"You were explaining to me why you use humour as a shield," I say, ignoring him.

"I was?"

"Yes, you were."

He sighs. "I don't like to show people the real me."

"Why not?"

"Because then it doesn't hurt as much when they decide to leave. I don't take it as personal."

"Why would they leave?"

"Because they always do. Trust me, it's been a reoccurring theme in my life."

He follows me over to the lift. "I'm sorry to hear that. Sometimes people don't realise what they've got until it's gone."

"That's very true." The doors open and he gestures for me to step inside. "After you. Which floor are you on?"

"The third."

"The same as me. How *convenient.*" He punches the button for the third floor and then we wait for the doors to close. I don't know if it's because we're in a confined space but the air shifts. Even though we're both silent, the sexual tension is deafening. We turn to face each other and it's obvious that we both feel it. "Hi," he says, his voice noticeably huskier than before.

"Hi."

"You know, if this was a scene out of a book or a movie, we would totally make out now."

I laugh. "It's a shame this is real life then."

"You're right, it is a shame." He takes a step closer to me. Two steps. Three. We're so close now. Too close. "I would pick you up, pin you against the wall and..."

The elevator shakes and then stops abruptly. I reach out and hold on to Jackson to steady myself. "What's happening?" I ask nervously as the lights above us begin to flicker.

"I think we might be stuck in here." He strokes his beard, pretending to be deep in thought. "I wonder what we could do to pass the time."

I can hear him talking but I can't make out any of the actual words. The only thing I can concentrate on is the four walls closing in on us. I feel the panic starting to bubble up inside of me as bile rises up my throat. I lean over and push a number of different buttons on the control panel to no avail. *Why isn't the call button working?*

Jackson laughs. "Why don't you press a few more for good measure? And I'm totally okay with your breasts pressing up against my arm, by the way." My breathing becomes quicker, heavier. I take a step backwards. "Hey, are you okay? I was only joking. I'm sorry if I've offended you."

"I'm claustrophobic," I tell him, feeling lightheaded. His face turns serious just before I close my eyes. "I think I'm about to have a panic attack."

"No you're not," he says, firm enough to make my eyes pop open. His are soft now. Soft, yet focused. "Keep looking at me, you hear me? Look straight into my eyes and listen to every word I say. Got it?"

I swallow hard. "Yes," I whisper in response.

"You've got this, Zara. You've. Got. This. You're bigger and better than the fear. You're in complete control. Take some deep breaths with me. Are you ready?" I nod. "Breathe in through your nose and out through your mouth." I do as he says. "Good. Again." I'm not sure how many times we do it but before long, I don't feel so lightheaded anymore. "Do you want to sit down?" I nod again. "Slowly," he tells me as we lower ourselves to the floor. He sits down opposite me, his legs on either side of mine. He shuffles closer and rests his hands on my bent knees. "Is this okay?"

It's more than okay. "Yes."

"Do you feel any better?"

"A little. Will you keep talking to me?"

"Of course." He takes a deep breath. "Do you ever get déjàvu?" I nod. "Well this is probably going to make me sound crazy but when I'm with you, it feels like I'm in a constant state of déjàvu. Even though we've only just met, you feel so familiar to me. It feels comfortable between us. Almost too comfortable. I can't shake the feeling that we've met before, or that we were always destined to meet. I realise how cheesy that sounds." He laughs nervously. "Hey, it's a good job we're stuck in this lift otherwise I'm pretty sure you would have run away by now."

I swallow hard, not a single ounce of panic or worry left in my body. "I won't run."

"You won't?"

"No, I won't."

"Good." He turns to face me and it feels like he doesn't just *look* at me but he *sees* me. "I agreed to answer your questions. Do you want to ask me anything else?"

I sit up a little straighter, not too sure how to broach the subject. "Um…my sister told me that your ex wrote a book about you."

He smiles sadly. "That's not a question."

"How do you feel about it?"

"I'm not going to lie, I was really hurt to begin with. It was hard to read."

"You read it?"

He nods. "I'm glad that I did. It was a great form of closure."

"How do you feel about everybody knowing your business?"

"It was strange at first but I don't even think about it anymore. To be honest, I think a lot of readers still see it as fiction."

"Why don't you take a cut of the money?"

"I don't want a dime off her. I don't want *anything* off her."

Hearing him say those words makes me happier than it probably should. "Why did you break up?"

"Your sister didn't tell you?"

"She only told me the basics."

"About five months ago, I came over here to work. Things weren't great when I left but I naïvely thought that some distance might help. Turns out I was wrong."

"What happened?"

"She met somebody else not long after I left."

"So she broke things off?"

"No. She fucked him for a few weeks first before telling me. She wanted me to go home so that we could sort everything out."

"And did you?"

"No, Zara, I didn't go back." The lift suddenly jolts and a few seconds later, we start to move. He smiles. "Is it bad that I wanted to be trapped with you for a little longer?" My heart starts to beat faster as he helps me to my feet. "Same time tomorrow?"

I laugh. "No, thanks." I breathe a huge sigh of relief as soon as the doors open.

"What's your room number?"

I raise my eyebrow. "Three one five."

"You're joking."

"I'm not."

He groans. "You shouldn't have told me."

"Why not?"

"Because now I'm going to be lying awake all night thinking about you in bed on the other side of the wall to me. And to tease me even more, the hotel went a put a connecting door between our rooms."

I laugh. "Good thing it's locked. I sleep naked."

He groans and places a hand over his heart. "You're killing me."

We stop when we reach our rooms. "Well...here we are."

His eyes twinkle. "Yes, here we are."

"Thanks for walking me back...and for helping me in the lift. I really appreciate it."

"No problem at all. It was my pleasure to help. You were really brave back there."

"Thank you." There's a long pause as we both wait for the other one to say something. I clear my throat. "Are you going back downstairs?"

"No, I only went down there to look for you."

"Oh, I thought you were joking."

Out of nowhere, my hotel door flies open and Halle stares at us, wide eyed. "Oh...Jackson...wow...I mean, hi. What...why...hi."

He chuckles. "Hey. I'm guessing you're Zara's sister?"

"Yes. I heard noises and came to see what it was. I ordered room service and they forgot to send part of my order up so they resent it but it was the wrong thing so I'm still waiting for it but I'm tired and why am I still talking?" She blushes.

"Well I've just come to drop your sister off safely." I feel his hand at the small of my back. "See you tomorrow?" I nod. "Sweetdreams, Zara." He grins. "You know where I am if you need me."

"Goodnight, Jackson."

As soon as the door closes behind me, Halle pulls on my arm and hisses, "I need details. Now!"

Chapter Four

The next morning, I almost blind myself with my eyeliner when the hotel phone rings. "Hello?" I answer.

"I heard you last night," Jackson says in greeting.

"I'm sorry, what?"

"I heard you through the wall. You were moaning and calling out my name all night long."

I roll my eyes. "In your dreams."

"I think you'll find that *I* was the one in *your* dreams."

"I'm busy, is there something that you want?"

"I think you know what I want, Zara." His gravelly voice sends a shiver down my spine.

"I'm going." *Before I take the shortest walk known to mankind to his room and make us both late for the signing.*

"Wait. I'm outside your door."

"Well that doesn't sound creepy in the slightest." I look down at the phone. "It says you're calling me from your room?"

"Go and look outside. You can thank me later."

I do as he says and laugh when I see one of his calendars propped up against the opposite wall. It's open on the month of July, which has an Independence Day theme. He has an American flag draped over his shoulders and a firework covering his manhood. *An extremely large firework.* There's a handwritten message underneath.

"Zara - fancy a bang?"

I can't help but grin. This man is a bad influence.

I like it.

***

One of the things I've quickly learned about book signings – you queue up. A lot. It's like Disney World on crack. If you think Disney fans are hardcore, you've seen nothing until you queue up with a group of romance readers discussing their favourite book boyfriend. I had no idea who Mason Hunter was until today but now I'm certain I want to marry him and have his babies. I'm number six in yet another queue when Halle walks up to me. "Hey, I can take over now. I've finished up my list already."

"That was quick," I reply.

"Yeah, I got chatting to one of the authors in the toilets and she signed my books in there so I didn't have to queue up."

I laugh. "How lovely…and hygienic."

"I've just seen Jackson leave the room for his lunch break. Why don't you go and grab something to eat with him?"

"Stop it."

"Stop what?"

"You're plotting."

She gasps. "Would I do that?"

"Yes. You're treating us like characters in one of your books. This is real life. I'm sweaty, I need a wee and my back is aching. There's nothing romantic about today's lunch break."

"You could at least play along."

I pass her the book that I'm holding and point to her trolley. "Mind the books. I'm going to chase after the man of my dreams. I need to declare my undying love for him before it's too late. I've been waiting my whole life for someone like Jacks to come along and now that he has, I can't let him go. I *won't* let him go."

Somebody clears their throat behind me. I slowly turn around and sure enough come face to face with Jackson.

Kill. Me. Now.

He grins. "The man of your dreams, huh?"

"I was joking."

"Stop trying to fight it."

I roll my eyes. "Tell him I was joking, Halle."

"I don't know what you mean," she replies, looking smug. "We were having a serious conversation."

"Oh, of course you're on his team. Thanks for the loyalty."

"It sounds like *you're* on my team, too," Jackson says. "In fact, I think I'll make you team captain."

"Remind me why I agreed to come and help you this weekend?" I ask Halle.

"So that you could declare your undying love for me," Jackson replies.

I curse Elouise for cancelling as I walk away from them both. Jackson quickly catches up to me. "I like it when you call me Jacks."

"Well that *is* your name," I tell him.

"You usually call me Jackson. Jacks sounds more familiar. I like it."

"Remind me to call you Jackson from now on then."

"Don't be like that. You've been waiting your whole life for someone like me, remember?" I ignore him and carry on walking. "Where are we going?"

"*I'm* going to the toilet."

"Cool. I'll come with you."

"And do what, exactly?"

His eyes dance with amusement. "I'd be more than happy to take off your jeans."

My heart starts to beat a little faster. I can't deny the effect he has on me. I spin around to face him. "Wait here, *Jackson*."

"Aww, do I have to?"

"Yes, you do."

I hear somebody ask him to sign their T-shirt as the door closes behind me. I take my time freshening myself up for the afternoon session so I don't expect him to be waiting for me when I walk out. "I missed you," he tells me.

Why is it that I spend most of my time rolling my eyes whenever I'm around him? "I thought you'd be too busy signing T-shirts to miss me."

"Where are we going for lunch?"

"*We?*"

"Yes. What are you in the mood for?" He wiggles his eyebrows up and down.

"I'm just going to grab a sandwich from the restaurant."

"I need some fresh air before going back in there. Will you come out with me? I'm American."

"And?"

"And I still don't know how things work over here."

"That's a crappy excuse. You've been here for five months."

"I'm being serious. I keep trying to tip people and make conversation with them but it doesn't go down too well."

"Just talk about the weather. We're good at that."

When we reach the hotel lobby, he points outside. "Oh look, it's raining cats and dogs."

I burst out laughing. "Was that supposed to be a British accent?"

"Why, yes, milady. One has been practicing one's accent."

"Well you need to practice more. *A lot* more."

He holds the door open for me. "Come for lunch with me. You can help me practice." I pause, considering my options. "What are you waiting for?" he asks in an Australian accent.

I can't help but laugh as I walk out of the door.

***

"What the hell is this?" he asks pointing to his tray.

"It's a Manchester egg," I tell him as we walk out of the pub.

"Say what?"

"It's a pickled egg coated in black pudding and sausage meat."

"And then deep fried?"

"Yep."

"I thought us Americans were the only ones to deep fry everything. This isn't what I had in mind."

"You're the one who said you wanted to try something traditional."

"Maybe next time we can have a traditional roast dinner or afternoon tea."

"Next time?"

"Yes. For our second date."

"*Date?*"

"Are you just going to copy everything that I say in a high-pitched voice?"

I scowl at him. "Are you going to have a taste or what?"

He grins. "Oh yes, I intend to have a taste *very* soon."

I pick it up and shove it into his mouth. He bites a piece off and puts the rest back onto his tray. "Mmmmm," he moans. "It tastes delicious, just like I knew it would." I shake my head, reading between the lines.

"What do you really think of it?"

"It's disgusting."

I laugh and hold out my hand. "I'll have it if you don't want it."

He goes to place it in my hand but then quickly pushes it into my mouth, like I did to him. "Mmmmm," I moan, teasing him. His eyes darken and he stands up a little straighter. "Soooo good. Just how I like it."

He sighs and takes the rest of it away from me. "Well that backfired," he says, before eating the rest of it in one bite. He swallows then grimaces. "You shouldn't be allowed to make those kinds of noises in public. Especially not in front of me."

"What?" I ask innocently. "I was just enjoying my lunch."

"It sounded like you were enjoying it a little too much."

"Aww, are you jealous of a little egg?"

"Of course not. You've been waiting your whole life to meet someone like me, remember?" I ignore him and pop a chip into my mouth. "What did you think of your little gift this morning?"

I raise my eyebrow. "I *think* the huge firework was unnecessary."

He laughs. "Oh, it was totally necessary. They had to buy the biggest one in the shop to make sure my own rocket was covered."

"Hmmmm, whatever you say."

"I can prove it to you, if you don't believe me."

I hold my hands up. "Okay, I believe you."

"Good." We walk in silence for a few seconds until he turns to me. "Do you actually believe me? Because you're going to be a little disappointed."

I laugh. "Don't worry. I won't ever be seeing your *rocket* so how could I be disappointed?"

"You should know that if you're playing hard to get, I love the chase."

"I'm not playing anything."

"Oookay."

"Don't say it like that."

"Okay," he says with a smug face.

"Stop it!"

"What? I'm just saying okay."

"You're not just saying okay, you're saying *okay*."

He laughs. "Um, okay?"

"Okay."

We walk in silence for a few minutes, eating our lunch before we need to head back inside. "Are you *okay*?" he asks, which makes us both laugh.

"Yes. Are you okay?"

"I'm more than okay. I've been fed and I have a beautiful woman by my side. Oh, crumbs. It's starting to rain again, milady. We should get back inside."

I giggle. "Still Australian."

Chapter Five

A couple of hours later, I face-plant onto the hotel bed. "I'm *so* tired."

"I can't hear you," Halle replies.

I somehow manage to lift my head up. "I'm knackered. Book signings are hard work."

She grins. "Yeah but they're worth it."

Seeing her so happy makes *me* happy. "Definitely."

"I'm looking forward to letting my hair down at the after-party later."

"I'll probably sleep through the whole thing."

She laughs. "So all it took was a few books to finally break you, hey?"

"A few? Try one hundred and nineteen. I counted. You need to be put on a book buying ban."

She gasps. "Don't even joke about that kind of thing."

"It won't be a joke when you're on one of those TV hoarder programmes when you're an old lady. You won't even be able to get into your bedroom because the books will be piled so high."

"That's the dream. Or better yet, to live in a house *made* of books."

"You need to go to bookaholics anonymous."

"Wait, does that actually exist?"

"I don't know but it should."

"That sounds like a fun way to spend my Friday night. I bet the hardcore readers would have some awesome recommendations."

I laugh. "That sounds exactly like something an addict would say."

She stands up straighter. "Hello, my name is Halle and I'm a bookaholic." She looks at her watch. "Ooops! I need to start getting ready. We're going for dinner in an hour. Are you coming?"

"Nah, I'm just going to stay here and chill for a bit. I might read something seeing as though it's like a library in here."

Her eyes nearly pop out of her head. "You're going to read?"

I shrug. "Maybe."

"What are you in the mood for?"

"A book, Halle."

"What kind of book?"

"I have no idea. I'll just browse."

"Um, no. I'm getting in on this. I've been trying to get you to read for years."

"Pfft, I read."

"Instagram captions don't count."

"Shut up and show me your books," I say as I roll off the bed.

"With pleasure." She opens one of her suitcases. "These are the books we got signed yesterday. Please be careful with them."

"What do you think I'm going to do?"

"I'm not sure. Just don't do anything crazy like fold the pages or spill water on them."

"I'm not going to vandalise your books."

"Do you want Young Adult, New Adult or Contemporary Romance?" I shouldn't have said anything. I should have just waited until she left and then looked for myself. She starts to rummage through the suitcase, and by rummage, what I actually mean is she carefully removes books from their bubble wrap pouches before stroking them. "What about The Honey Trap? It's about this kickass heroine who exposes cheating men. I actually need a re-read of it soon."

"It sounds great but I wanted something more…" *Jackson.*

She laughs. "Ah, I think I know what you're trying to say."

"You do?" She's always been extremely insightful.

"Yes." A moment later she hands me a book and winks. "Try this one. It's *very* steamy."

"Oh. Oh, no. I didn't mean...*that*. I was going to ask if you had the book with Jackson in it."

"Jackson as in Jackson Price?" I nod. "No. I didn't bring it because his ex isn't a signing author."

"It's fine. No big deal."

"Why do you want to read about him?"

"I'm just interested."

"In his story or in him?"

"His story. I want to see what all the fuss is about." I already *know* what the fuss is about. He has an addictive personality. And face.

"You can read it when we get home. Unless you download the eBook onto your phone." She lowers her voice. "There's been a rumour going around about his ex."

"What about her?"

"Apparently around the time they broke up, her book sales weren't doing very well."

"And?"

"And she needed some inspiration...so she caused some drama in her real life."

"Are you saying that she cheated on Jackson for the sake of a plotline?"

"Well she didn't cheat on him but yes..."

"She *did* cheat on him. Jackson told me. She was sleeping with the other guy for weeks before she came clean."

Her eyes go wide. "He told you that?"

"Yes. There's always two sides to every story."

"Jesus. I guess she didn't want to come across as the villain."

"Don't tell anybody. Jackson told me in confidence."

"I won't. I wonder why he doesn't want people to know the truth about her?"

Because he's a good person. "What would he gain from it? He just wants to move on with his life." She winces. "What was that look for?"

"She's writing a sequel, I don't think he's going to get away from it any time soon."

"Well at least Jackson won't be in it. He's been over here for the past five months."

"Maybe she's waiting for him to return. I think her readers want to know if they're going to get back together." My heart sinks at the thought. "It's all just rumours anyway. Jackson's a big boy, I'm sure he will make the right decision. Okay, I really need to start getting ready." She points at her suitcase. "Look after my babies."

As soon as she leaves the room, I close the suitcase and lie back down on the bed. I'm not in the mood to read, especially when the line between real life and fiction has become so blurred.

Chapter Six

I wake up to somebody knocking on the door. I jump up too fast and have to hold onto the wall until my head stops spinning.

"I know you're in there," I hear Jackson say. "I can hear you calling out my name again."

I open the door to see him casually leaning against the door frame, like he's on a photo shoot or a movie set. He could easily pass as a movie star. He's ridiculously handsome and has the swagger to match. "Did I wake you?"

"Yes. What time is it and why are you here?"

He laughs. "It's nice to see you too, Zara. It's eight o'clock and I've come to pick you up for the after-party."

"Pick me up? You're staying in the room next door. You're hardly picking me up."

"For your information, I've already been down to the party. When I couldn't find you, I asked your sister where you were and came back up here. That's when I heard your moans."

"I'm sorry, I just can't seem to stop dreaming about you," I say as I look down at my jeans and converse. "I'm not dressed."

He raises his eyebrow. "Trust me, I wouldn't be standing out here if you weren't dressed."

I try not to blush. "You know what I mean. I'm not dressed to party."

"You look beautiful."

"I'll just get changed quickly."

"Okay, I can help."

"You can *help* by waiting right there."

"Aww, are you really going to make your date wait outside?"

"My date?"

"Yes. You should probably know that I kiss on the second date."

I roll my eyes and gesture for him to come inside. "You can wait in here. I'll get ready in the bathroom."

"Oh, so *now* you invite me inside, now you know that I put out. Which one's your bed?"

I point to the one on the right. "I'll be five minutes. No funny business."

He laughs. "What exactly do you class as funny business?"

"I don't know…sniffing my underwear or something weird like that."

"Don't worry. I don't do that until the third date."

***

"I still can't believe you keep my calendar in bed with you," Jackson says as I take a sip of my second cocktail of the evening.

"I don't *keep it* in bed with me. It was *on* the bed because that's where I left it this morning."

"Come on, Zara. Just admit that you want me in your bed." His eyes light up when the next song comes on. He stands up and holds his hand out. "Dance with me."

"What? Why?"

He chuckles. "Because I want to dance with you. And because this is one of my all-time favourite songs."

"I don't even know what it is."

"It's *Def Leppard*. Come on."

"I'm not drunk yet."

"Good. I want you to remember everything." His bedroom eyes burn into mine and Jesus, I'd do just about anything he asked me to right now. He grins when I stand up and leads me over to the dance floor. I lose count of the number of women who turn to watch us or whisper as we walk by.

"Okay then, let's see your moves, Jackson Price."

His eyes twinkle as he lifts our entwined hands up in the air and slowly spins me around until I'm facing away from him. He lets our hands drop and waits a few seconds, building the anticipation, before taking hold of my hips and pulling me back so that our bodies are flush. "I intend on showing you *every single one* of my moves." I swallow hard as he starts to move in time with the music. We quickly find our own rhythm and in a matter of seconds, we're moving as one. It's as though our bodies are jigsaw pieces, designed to fit together perfectly. Heat rushes to my cheeks, and other body parts, as I allow myself to imagine what it would be like to have our own private after-party. It becomes obvious that we're thinking along the same lines when I feel something hard pressing into my back. He brings his mouth down to my neck and places a gentle kiss, followed by a flick of his tongue. Blame it on the heat of the moment, or the music, or the alcohol, but I turn around, desperate to feel more of him. His eyes turn dark as I stand on my tiptoes and begin to slowly grind up against him. I don't care where we are or who is watching. All that matters in this moment is us. He leans in even closer and just when I think he's about to kiss me, the song comes to an end. We stay pressed up against each other for a few more seconds, basking in the moment, until the lighting changes and an upbeat song begins to play.

He smiles at me, his eyes now glazed. "Well I think it's safe to say that was the most fun I've ever had with my clothes on."

I laugh. "You have some impressive moves."

"Baby, that was just the warm up."

This man is going to be the death of me. "Hey, I'll be back in a minute."

"Where are you going?"

"The ladies' room."

"Oh, I get it. You're dumping me now you've had what you want."

Trust me, I haven't had what I want. Not yet. "I need to freshen up."

He laughs. "But I like you all hot and sweaty."

"I bet you do." I let go of his hand and it immediately feels as though something is missing.

"I'll be waiting for you."

"You better," I tell him as I walk away.

Halle quickly falls into step beside me. "Um, okay, so when are we going to talk about the fact that you just dry humped Jackson Price in front of hundreds of people?"

"We were just dancing."

"*Dirty* dancing. I might have to start calling you Baby. What's going on with you two?"

"Nothing."

"Okay, you keep telling yourself that."

"He lives in America, Halle."

"And?"

"And I'd prefer to have a boyfriend who lives in the same country as me, thanks."

She claps excitedly. "I didn't mention anything about a boyfriend. You really do like him, don't you?"

"Shhhh," I tell her as I open the door to the toilets. "Keep your voice down."

"I knew he was your type."

"I don't have a type."

"Yes you do. Tall, blonde hair and beards." *She has a point.* "I'm sure you two could make it work."

"Woah, you're getting way too ahead of yourself. He might not even be interested."

"I saw how he was holding you on the dance floor. He's definitely interested."

"Maybe he's looking for a one night stand. Maybe I'd just be some kind of rebound to him."

"Do you really believe that?"

I sigh. "No."

"Don't shut him out, Zar. Don't let your past ruin your future. He seems like a really good guy *and* he's awesome in bed."

"How the hell would you know?"

"It's in Nicole's book."

"I'm guessing Nicole is his ex."

She nods. "Let's just say that she's a very *descriptive* writer."

Now I definitely don't want to read it. Why would you ever write so candidly about your own life? Your own *sex life*?

The door opens and a group of women walk in, one of which recognises Halle. They begin to talk about books, which is my cue to leave.

I walk back into the main room and immediately spot Jackson at the bar. He's talking to another cover model but grins as soon as he sees me. Without taking his eyes off mine, he excuses himself and slowly saunters towards me, a knowing look in his eye. The air feels charged and it's obvious that we both know where all of this is heading. I smile back at him and take a step forward when a woman steps in front of him, cutting me off. I stop, my face only inches away from the back of her head. I step to the side and notice Jackson's wide eyes. "What are you doing here, Nicole?" he asks.

Nicole. My heart sinks.

"I'm here for you. Can we go somewhere a little more private?"

"No, we can't."

I'm frozen to the spot, unable to move but wishing more than anything that I could. I have no desire to hear what she has to say.

"I flew all this way just to see you."

"Why? Because you need some more book material? Have you run out of inspiration back home? I heard you're writing a sequel. Will you write about tonight? Are you going to tell the truth this time? We're over, Nicole. We were over five months ago." His eyes find mine and I see a mixture of disappointment, frustration and regret all at once. "I'm sorry," he says to me.

She turns to face me. "Who are you?"

"Leave her out of it," Jackson answers.

"I think I should go," I tell him, a crowd starting to form close by.

"No," Jackson says. "Please stay. We're done here. There's nothing more to say."

"I have a lot more to say," Nicole replies. "I still love you, Jackson."

He runs a hand through his hair. "No, you don't. Why haven't you tried to contact me in the last five months? Why did you have to fly over here to tell me? Stop with the theatrics. I don't want to be a part of your fucked-up storylines anymore. This is real life, Nicole. Stop trying to live inside the pages of a book."

She gestures to me. "Are you and her together? Is that what all of this is about?"

"Even if I had never met Zara, I would still be saying the exact same thing to you right now." He looks straight at me and says with one hundred percent sincerity, "If I had my own way then yes, we would be together."

I don't even know how to feel right now. All I know is that I want to leave. "You need to sort this out between the two of you."

"Please don't leave," he tells me.

"It's all too much. I'm sorry." I turn away and walk out of the room as quickly as I can, taking deep breaths as I go. In the space of a few days, I've gone from being single to meeting the perfect guy who just so happens to live in another country. And to top it all off, he has an ex-girlfriend who is still in love with him. *Why is it always me?*

I'm about to push the button for the lift when I hear my name being called. I turn around to see Jackson chasing after me. "Please don't leave. I want to spend as much time with you as possible."

"Why?"

"If you haven't figured it out yet, I kind of have a thing for you."

"I'm being serious. Why me?"

"Why *not?* You're perfect. You're everything I could ever want in a woman. You're beautiful, and smart, and funny, and opinionated, and selfless, and you're a smart ass but I'm already addicted to you."

"Jackson…I don't do messy."

"Me neither."

"So then what are we doing here? You live in America."

"My visa doesn't run out for another month."

"One month is nothing."

"If this is about Nicole then I can assure you…"

"It's not just about her. Even if she wasn't in the picture, you still live in America."

"And? You make it sound like I'm from a different planet."

"Long distance doesn't work."

"*Long distance* might not work but *we* will."

"You can't say that. You can't *know* that."

"Yes I can. We would work, Zara. Trust me."

"Please don't make promises that you can't keep."

"I would never do that to you."

"But how the hell can you be so sure? You've only known me for two days."

"And? This has been one of the best weekends of my life, thanks to you. Plus, everybody has a day two."

"What are you talking about?"

"Every single couple in the entire history of the universe had to meet for the first time at some point. They all had a day one, and a day two, and a day three. Long-lasting relationships aren't created on the spot. They take time and hard work. This might only be our day two but I'm positive there's going to be more. Why don't we take each day as it comes? If we reach day three or day thirty three or day *three hundred and thirty three* and you decide that you don't want this then fine, but just give us a chance. Don't rule this out before it's even started."

"But what about when you leave? I'd rather be hurt on day two than day twenty two or thirty two."

"Zara, be honest with me. Do you not feel what I feel? Because I *think* you do but if I've read this all wrong then I'll walk away and just feel lucky to have even met you."

I pause, thinking very carefully about what I want. I realise that the next few words out of my mouth could have a major impact on my life. I lace my fingers in between his. "I feel it."

Relief floods his face. "So what do you say? Do you want to try day three? And the rest?"

I grin. "Let's do it."

"I'm going to kiss you now." He takes my face in both of his hands and kisses me like there's no tomorrow. And in this moment, there isn't. There's only us. Right here. Right now.

Epilogue

Jackson

Day Thirty

"Hey, don't cry. I'll see you in a little over a month, remember?"

"I know but it doesn't make it any easier to say goodbye today. I've been glued to your hip for the past four weeks."

I wiggle my eyebrows up and down. "You've been glued to *something*."

"I'm going to miss you and your dirty mind."

I wrap my arms around her and kiss the top of her head. "I'll miss you too but it'll be Christmas before we know it. I can't wait to introduce you to my family. My Mom is going to love you." I lean down and whisper in her ear, "But not as much as I do."

She pulls away and looks up at me with teary eyes. "You do?"

"Yes. I love you, Zara."

Her grin threatens to take over her entire face. "I love you too, Jacks."

I breathe a huge sigh of relief that we're on the same page. I never in my wildest dreams thought that I would meet my happy ever after at a book signing of all places.

Thank fuck for books.

The End.

About the Author

Karli Perrin is a twenty something, English Language and Linguistics graduate from Manchester, England. She has always been a big lover of books and was inspired to write her debut novel in 2013. She is a huge believer of fate and is a sucker for a happy ending. Her ultimate goal in life is to live in a house made entirely out of books with her fiancé and two children.

...Hogwarts is plan B.

11391763R00025

Printed in Great Britain
by Amazon